The Nice Dream Truck

The Nice Dr

For Ally, who fearlessly chases her dreams—B.F.

To Robin—B.B.

eam Truck

by Beth Ferry

illustrated by Brigette Barrager

HARPER

An Imprint of HarperCollinsPublishers

When bedtime is near
and teeth are all brushed
and the house is asleep
and the noises are hushed,

you might hear a tune.

You might be in luck.

You might get a visit from the Nice Dream Truck.

The truck is a wonder.

It floats and it flies,

steered by a girl with stars in her eyes

who's ready to help you

get ready for bed

by serving up dreams to dream in your head.

The choices are endless.

The toppings? Worth trying!

They're silly and funny and SO satisfying—

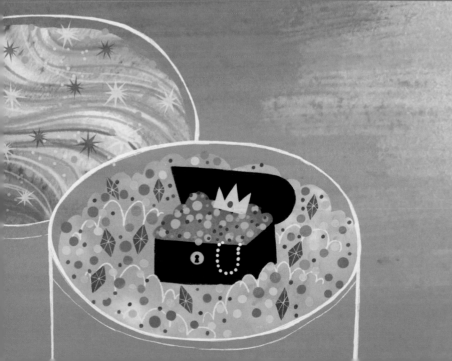

with dreams about treasure

and dreams about winning.

Dreams about magic

and pirouette spinning.

Dreams about summer
and dreams about snow.

Dreams about puppies
wherever you go.

Sample some princess!
Try super speed!

Or be the great hero who helps those in need.

Dream about flying.

Dream about whales.

Dream about dragons
with jelly bean scales.

Scoop up some moonbeams!

Try astronaut!

Or the triple-dip cone
that's called making the shot.

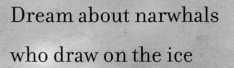

Dream about narwhals
who draw on the ice

or years where your birthday
comes not once but *twice*.

And if you like dreams a tiny bit scary,
dream of sea monsters, hefty and hairy.

Sample some drummer.

Taste some guitar.

Try standing ovation

or even rock star.

There are dreams that are big
and dreams that are small

and dreams where the kids are in charge of it all.

Dreams that surprise
and dreams that delight
and dreams so supreme
you'll choose them each night.

So pile your dish with scoops to the sky
or choose just the one you've been longing to try.

There's all kinds of dreams
for all kinds of kids.
Try something new!
You'll be glad that you did.

So scope out your choices.

Make up your mind.

Hold out your bowl and get ready to find

a dish full of dreams that was scooped just for you

by this magical pair who make dreams come true.

Now hop into bed and snuggle down deep.

You've got your nice dream.

Good night . . .

Time to sleep.